Against All Odds: A Novel of Triumph and Perseverance

Jane Stephens

Published by RWG Publishing, 2023.

This is a work of fiction. Similarities to real people, places, or events are entirely coincidental.

AGAINST ALL ODDS: A NOVEL OF TRIUMPH AND PERSEVERANCE

First edition. January 25, 2023.

Copyright © 2023 Jane Stephens.

Written by Jane Stephens.

Table of Contents

Chapter 1: The Beginning of the Struggle 1
Chapter 2: Doubt and Despair 3
Chapter 3: A Ray of Hope 5
Chapter 4: The Road to Redemption 7
Chapter 5: The Climb to Success 9
Chapter 6: The Price of Victory 13
Chapter 7: The Darkest Hour 15
Chapter 8: The Turning Point 19
Chapter 9: The Power of Persistence 21
Chapter 10: Overcoming Adversity 25
Chapter 11: The Final Push 27
Chapter 12: The Triumph of the Human Spirit 29
Chapter 13: The Aftermath of Victory 33
Chapter 14: The Legacy of Perseverance 37
Chapter 15: The Future of Triumph 41

Chapter 1: The Beginning of the Struggle

The main character, Jane, sat at her desk staring blankly at the blank page in front of her. She had been trying to write her novel for months, but nothing seemed to come to her. She was tired, broke and feeling like a complete failure. Her dream of becoming a published author seemed to be slipping away with each passing day.

Jane had always loved writing and had been working on her novel for years, but life had a way of getting in the way. She had been struggling to make ends meet, working two jobs to pay the bills and support herself. With so little time and energy to devote to her writing, she had been unable to make any real progress.

She had been working as a waitress at a local diner during the day and as a cashier at a convenience store at night. The long hours and low pay took a toll on her, both physically and mentally. She was exhausted, but she couldn't afford to quit either of her jobs.

The rejections from publishers and literary agents only added to her feelings of hopelessness. She had been told that her writing wasn't good enough, that her story was too cliché and that she would never make it as a writer. She felt like she had hit rock bottom and didn't know how to pick herself back up.

Feeling defeated, Jane decided to take a break from writing and focus on her day jobs. She knew she needed to make some money if she was going to be able to continue working on her novel. She put her manuscript in a drawer and tried to forget about it.

But the dream of being a published author was too strong to ignore. She knew that she couldn't give up on her dream just because it was hard. She decided to take her manuscript out of the drawer and start working on it again.

With renewed determination, Jane set to work revising and editing her novel. She spent countless hours pouring over every word, trying to make it the best it could be. She knew that it wasn't going to be easy, but she was determined to see it through. She would work on it during her breaks at work, and late into the night after she returned home.

She also decided to take a creative writing class at a local college to improve her skills and gain more insight into the publishing industry. It was difficult to balance her day jobs and school work but she knew it would be worth it in the end.

Despite all the struggles and setbacks, Jane never gave up. She knew that the road to success would be long and difficult, but she was willing to fight for her dream. She would read the rejection letters from publishers and agents and use them as motivation to improve her craft.

This was the beginning of her journey, the beginning of the struggle. Jane knew that it wouldn't be easy, but she was determined to see it through. She was ready to face whatever challenges came her way, because she knew that the reward at the end would be worth it.

Chapter 2: Doubt and Despair

Jane's determination to finish her novel was met with a new set of challenges. As she worked on her manuscript, she began to doubt her abilities as a writer. She read and reread her work, constantly second-guessing herself. She found herself questioning whether her story was truly worth telling, and if anyone would even want to read it.

The constant rejections from publishers and literary agents didn't help matters. They only served to reinforce her doubts and make her question her worth as a writer. She felt like she was stuck in a never-ending cycle of self-doubt and despair.

The stress of her day jobs and the added pressure of schoolwork didn't help either. She was struggling to make ends meet and was constantly exhausted. She found it difficult to focus on her writing and often felt too drained to work on her manuscript.

The weight of her struggles was starting to take a toll on her mental health. She found herself feeling hopeless and alone. She didn't know how much longer she could keep going.

Despite her doubts and despair, Jane refused to give up. She knew that the road to success would be long and difficult, but she was determined to see it through. She reminded herself that every successful writer had faced rejection and self-doubt.

Jane decided to seek help, she sought the guidance of her creative writing teacher and also started attending a support group for aspiring authors. It was there that she met other writers who were going through similar struggles. They provided her with a sense of community and support.

She also began to read books and articles on the writing process and the struggles of being a writer. Reading about the experiences of other writers helped her to understand that her doubts and struggles were normal and that she was not alone.

Jane also began to make a conscious effort to take care of herself. She started to exercise, eat well and make time for herself. She knew that she couldn't pour from an empty cup and took steps to take care of her physical and mental well-being.

The journey was still difficult and uncertain, but Jane knew that she had to push through the doubt and despair. She knew that it was all part of the process and that the end goal was worth it. She kept moving forward, one step at a time, determined to see her dream of becoming a published author come true.

Chapter 3: A Ray of Hope

After months of hard work and perseverance, Jane finally received some good news. One of her short stories had been accepted for publication in a literary magazine. It was a small victory, but it was enough to give her a ray of hope. The magazine was a reputable one and had a wide readership, this was a huge milestone for her.

This acceptance letter was the first indication that her writing was good enough and that her story was worth telling. It was a sign that her hard work and determination were paying off. She felt a sense of validation and accomplishment that she had never felt before. It made all the struggles and rejections worth it, and it gave her the motivation to keep going.

The acceptance letter was also a reminder that she had a talent and a passion for writing, which she had almost lost sight of due to her doubts and struggles. It gave her the confidence to keep going, to continue working on her novel. She felt a renewed sense of excitement and purpose in her writing.

Jane also found a literary agent who was willing to take a chance on her novel. The agent was enthusiastic about her work and believed in her ability to be a successful author. This was a huge step towards her dream of being a published author. The agent provided her with guidance and resources that she had never had before, and it made the publishing process less daunting.

The support and encouragement from her agent helped to lift the weight of doubt and despair that Jane had been carrying for so long. She felt renewed and re-energized, ready to tackle whatever lay ahead. She felt like she had a team and a support system behind her, which made the journey less lonely and more manageable.

In addition to her writing career, Jane's personal life was also starting to look up. She was able to quit her second job and focus on her writing full-time. This was a big step for her as it allowed her to devote more time and energy to her craft. She also found a new, better paying job that allowed her more flexibility and better work-life balance.

With her financial struggles beginning to ease, Jane was finally able to breathe a little easier. She could focus on her writing and her personal growth without the constant stress and strain of making ends meet. She felt like she had more control over her life and her future.

This period was a turning point in Jane's journey. It was a ray of hope that reminded her that she was on the right path, that she was capable of achieving her dreams, and that the struggles she had faced were worth it. It was a reminder to her that there was light at the end of the tunnel, and that she was closer to her goal than ever before. With renewed confidence and determination, Jane knew that she was ready to take the next step and face whatever challenges lay ahead.

Chapter 4: The Road to Redemption

Jane had made significant progress in her writing career, but she still had a long way to go. The road to redemption was a challenging one, filled with obstacles and setbacks. She found herself facing new struggles and obstacles that she had never encountered before.

One of the biggest challenges Jane faced was the editing and rewriting process. Her agent provided her with detailed notes and feedback on her manuscript, which she had to incorporate into her work. It was a difficult process, and it was hard to let go of parts of her story that she had grown attached to. But she knew that the changes were necessary in order to make her story the best it could be.

Another obstacle Jane faced was the constant rejection from publishers. Despite her agent's best efforts, they were unable to secure a publishing deal for her novel. It was frustrating and disheartening to see her hard work and dedication not result in success.

The stress and disappointment took a toll on Jane's mental health. She found herself struggling with feelings of self-doubt and despair. She questioned whether she was cut out to be a writer, and if her dream of becoming a published author was ever going to become a reality.

However, Jane refused to give up. She knew that the road to redemption was a long and difficult one, but she was determined to see it through. She reminded herself that every successful writer had faced rejection and struggles. She also knew that the process of rewriting and editing her manuscript was an important part of making it the best it could be.

To keep herself motivated, Jane surrounded herself with a supportive community of writers. She also sought the guidance of her agent, who provided her with valuable feedback and encouragement.

Jane also began to practice self-care, making sure to take care of her physical and mental well-being. She made a conscious effort to exercise, eat well, and make time for herself. She realized that in order to be successful, she needed to be in a good place both physically and mentally.

The road to redemption was long and difficult, but Jane knew that it was necessary for her to grow as a writer and for her novel to be the best it could be. She kept moving forward, one step at a time, determined to see her dream of becoming a published author come true.

Chapter 5: The Climb to Success

After months of hard work and perseverance, Jane finally reached the summit of her journey. Her novel was accepted for publication by a reputable publisher. She had made it, she was going to be a published author. It was a dream come true and it felt surreal that all her hard work had paid off.

The climb to success was not an easy one, it was filled with obstacles, setbacks, and struggles. But Jane had pushed through, never giving up on her dream. She had faced her doubts and fears, and had come out on top. The journey had been a long and difficult one, but she knew that it had been necessary in order to reach this point.

The acceptance from the publisher was a validation of all her hard work and dedication. It was a recognition of her talent and a confirmation that her story was worth telling. She felt a sense of accomplishment and pride that she had never felt before. She called her family and friends to share the news, and it was a moment of joy and celebration for everyone.

The publishing process was not without its challenges, there were still a lot of revisions and editing to be done before the book was ready to be released. But Jane was excited to work on it, knowing that it was one step closer to her dream coming true. She went through the manuscript one more time, making changes and adjustments as per the publisher's notes. It was a tedious process but she was determined to make her book the best it could be.

The support and guidance of her agent and publisher were instrumental in the process. They provided her with the resources and expertise that she needed to take her novel to the next level. Her agent helped her negotiate her contract with the publisher and provided her with advice on how to navigate the publishing industry. Her publisher helped her with the cover design, marketing and promotion of her book. They provided her with a team of professionals to help her with the final stages of the publishing process.

The news of her upcoming publication brought a renewed sense of energy and excitement to Jane. She felt a renewed sense of purpose and passion for her writing. She was eager to share her story with the world and to see how it would be received. She started to prepare for book signings, events and interviews. It was a new experience for her, but she was ready to take it on.

The climb to success was not easy, but it was worth it. The struggles, setbacks and obstacles that Jane faced along the way had made her a better writer and a stronger person. She knew that the journey had been a necessary one, and that it had prepared her for the challenges that lay ahead. She had learned to face her fears, to overcome her doubts and to never give up on her dream.

Jane had finally reached the summit of her journey, but she knew that the climb to success was not over yet. With her book set to be released, she was ready to tackle whatever lay ahead and to continue to grow as a writer. She was excited for the next chapter of her journey and ready to see where it would take her.

It was a new beginning, and she was ready to see where this new path would lead her.

Chapter 6: The Price of Victory

Jane's novel was finally released, and it was met with great success. Her book was well-received by critics and readers alike, and it quickly climbed the bestseller charts. It was a dream come true for Jane, but it came with its own set of challenges and struggles.

The price of victory was high. Jane found herself caught up in a whirlwind of book signings, interviews, and events. She was constantly on the go, traveling to different cities and countries to promote her book. It was an exciting experience, but it also meant that she was away from home for long periods of time. She was exhausted, and she found it hard to keep up with the demands of her newfound fame. She missed her family and friends, and it was hard to maintain a sense of normalcy in her life.

The pressure of her success was also overwhelming. She was expected to produce a follow-up novel, and the pressure to come up with another hit was immense. The expectations were high, and she felt like she had to live up to them. She found herself struggling with writer's block and a lack of inspiration. She felt like she was stuck in a never-ending cycle of stress and pressure. She didn't want to disappoint her readers and her publisher.

The constant attention and scrutiny also took a toll on her personal life. She found it hard to maintain relationships and friendships, and she felt like she was losing touch with the people who mattered most to her. She was struggling to find a balance between her personal and professional life. She had to be careful of what she said and did, as she was aware that everything she did was being watched.

Despite the challenges and struggles that came with her success, Jane knew that it was all worth it. She had worked hard for this, and she was determined to make the most of it. She knew that the price of victory was high, but she was willing to pay it. She was grateful for the opportunity and wanted to make the most of it.

To cope with the demands of her success, Jane made a conscious effort to take care of herself. She made sure to get enough rest, exercise, and eat well. She also made time for herself, doing things she enjoyed and that helped her to relax. She started to meditate and practice yoga to help her cope with the stress.

She also sought the support and guidance of those closest to her. She opened up to her family and friends about her struggles, and they provided her with the support and understanding that she needed. They were her rock and helped her navigate through the challenges that came with her success.

The price of victory was high, but Jane knew that it was all worth it. She had achieved her dream, and she was determined to make the most of it. She was ready to face whatever challenges lay ahead and to continue to grow as a writer and as a person. She was determined to make the most of the opportunity, and to make her book the best it could be.

Chapter 7: The Darkest Hour

Jane's success as a published author was short-lived. Despite the initial success of her novel, it failed to maintain its spot on the bestseller lists. Sales began to decline, and her publisher and agent became increasingly distant and unresponsive.

This was a difficult time for Jane, as she felt like she had hit rock bottom. She had poured her heart and soul into her writing, and to see it fail was devastating. She felt like she had let down her readers, her publisher, and herself.

As the sales of her book continued to drop, her publisher dropped her from their list. Her agent also decided to part ways with her, citing her lack of sales as the reason. Jane found herself alone and without a support system.

The rejection and failure took a heavy toll on Jane's mental health. She struggled with feelings of worthlessness and failure. She had believed that her writing was her talent and her passion, and to see it fail was crushing. She found it hard to find motivation to write, and she was plagued by self-doubt and insecurity.

In addition to her professional struggles, Jane's personal life was also in turmoil. Her relationships with friends and family were strained, as they didn't understand her struggles or know how to help her. She felt isolated and alone.

This was the darkest hour for Jane. She felt like she had reached the end of her journey and that there was nowhere else to go. She felt like she had failed as a writer and as a person.

Despite the darkness, Jane refused to give up. She knew that she needed to find a way to pick herself up and move forward. She sought therapy, and it helped her to come to terms with her feelings and learn to cope with her struggles. She also found comfort in the support of her loved ones, who helped her to see that failure was not the end.

With the help of therapy and the support of her loved ones, Jane started to find her way back to her passion for writing. She started to write again, but this time, she wrote for herself and not for anyone else. She wrote for the love of it, and not for the validation of others.

This was the darkest hour for Jane, but it was also the beginning of a new chapter in her journey. She had hit rock bottom, but she had also found the strength to pick herself up and move forward. She realized that failure was not the end, it was an opportunity to learn and grow. She knew that she had to let go of the past and focus on the future.

Jane started to experiment with her writing, trying out different genres and styles. She discovered that she had a talent for writing poetry and started to publish her work online. She also started a blog, where she wrote about her experiences as a writer and shared her struggles and triumphs with her readers.

As she wrote and shared her work, she started to gain a following of readers who appreciated her honest and raw writing. They related to her struggles and felt a connection to her work. They encouraged her to keep writing and to never give up.

AGAINST ALL ODDS: A NOVEL OF TRIUMPH AND PERSEVERANCE

The darkest hour had passed, and Jane was once again on her way. She had found a new passion for writing and a new purpose in sharing her story. She had learned that failure was not the end, it was a stepping stone on the path to success. She was determined to keep moving forward, to keep learning and growing, and to never give up on her dream.

Chapter 8: The Turning Point

After months of struggling and trying to find her footing, Jane finally reached a turning point in her journey. She had been experimenting with different genres and styles of writing, and had found a new passion for poetry. She started to publish her work online and to her surprise, her poetry gained a following of readers who appreciated her honest and raw writing. They related to her struggles and felt a connection to her work.

This newfound success in poetry gave Jane a renewed sense of purpose and motivation. She had always believed that her writing was her talent and her passion, and to have found a new outlet for her creativity was a revelation. She felt a renewed sense of excitement and passion for writing that she had not felt in a long time.

As she continued to write and share her poetry, Jane started to gain recognition in the literary community. She was invited to poetry readings and events, where she had the opportunity to share her work with a wider audience. Her poetry was also featured in literary magazines and anthologies, which further increased her visibility and credibility as a writer.

This was a turning point for Jane, as she had found a new direction and purpose in her writing. Her success in poetry had also helped her to overcome her feelings of failure and rejection from her previous experience as a novelist. She had finally found her place in the literary world and she was determined to make the most of it.

In addition to her professional success, Jane's personal life also began to improve. Her relationships with friends and family had been strained due to her struggles, but now that she was finding success as a poet, they were able to understand and support her better. They were proud of her accomplishments and were happy to see her thriving and happy again.

Jane also realized that the struggles she faced as a novelist had been a valuable learning experience. She had learned to face her fears and overcome her doubts, and she had learned to never give up on her dream. She had learned to be resilient and to keep moving forward, even in the face of adversity.

This turning point marked a new beginning for Jane, both in her professional and personal life. She was excited for the future, and she was determined to continue to grow and evolve as a writer. She knew that the journey would not be easy, but she was ready to face whatever challenges lay ahead.

Jane had finally found her place in the literary world, and she was determined to make the most of it. The turning point marked the end of her struggles and the beginning of a new chapter in her journey. She was ready to take on the world and to share her story with the world.

Chapter 9: The Power of Persistence

Jane's newfound success as a poet was not without its own set of challenges and struggles. She had to work hard to maintain her visibility and credibility in the literary world, and she had to continuously produce new and exciting work to keep her readers engaged. She had to find ways to stand out in a crowded and competitive industry, where new voices are constantly emerging.

Despite the challenges, Jane persisted. She knew that the path to success was not easy and that it required hard work and dedication. She was determined to make the most of her opportunity and to prove to herself and others that she had what it takes to be a successful writer. She was determined to make a name for herself in the literary world and to leave a lasting impact.

She knew that the key to her success was persistence. She never gave up, even when faced with rejection or setbacks. She used them as learning opportunities and as motivation to improve her craft. She knew that it was important to keep pushing forward and to never give up on her dream. She also knew that it was important to keep learning and evolving as a writer, to stay relevant and to be open to new opportunities and collaborations.

Through her persistence, Jane was able to build a loyal following of readers who appreciated her honesty and vulnerability in her poetry. Her poetry was relatable and touched on themes that were relevant to her readers. She had a unique voice and style, and her readers found comfort and inspiration in her work. She was able to connect with her readers on a personal level, and they felt like they knew her through her poetry.

Her persistence also paid off in her professional life. She was invited to more and more poetry readings, events and literary festivals. She was also offered collaborations and opportunities to teach and mentor young writers. Her persistence had helped her to establish herself as a respected and successful poet in the literary community. She had gained the respect of her peers and was considered as a role model for many aspiring writers.

Jane also realized that the power of persistence was not limited to her professional life. She had also applied it to her personal life, she had worked hard to repair her relationships with friends and family, and to find balance in her life. She had learned that persistence was key to achieving her goals and to finding happiness and fulfillment in her life. She had learned to set boundaries, to communicate effectively and to prioritize her well-being.

The power of persistence had been a valuable lesson for Jane. She had learned that success was not easy, but it was achievable if you were willing to work hard and never give up. She was determined to continue to apply this lesson to her life and to inspire others to do the same. She wanted to use her experience and her success to empower others and to show them that with hard work and persistence, anything is possible.

In the end, Jane realized that the power of persistence was not just about achieving success, it was about the journey and the person she had become. She had learned to never give up on her dreams, to face her fears and to never let setbacks define her. She had become a stronger and more resilient person, and she was proud of all that she had accomplished.

The power of persistence had helped Jane to achieve her dream and to find her place in the literary world. She knew that the journey would not be easy, but she was ready to face whatever challenges lay ahead, with the determination and persistence that had brought her this far. She was proud of the person she had become and she was excited for what the future held.

Chapter 10: Overcoming Adversity

Jane's journey as a writer had not been easy. She had faced many challenges and obstacles along the way, but she had learned to overcome adversity. She had learned that success was not guaranteed, and that it required hard work, dedication, and the ability to rise above challenges and setbacks.

One of the biggest challenges Jane faced was the rejection and failure of her first novel. It was a difficult time for her, as she had poured her heart and soul into her writing, and to see it fail was devastating. She felt like she had let down her readers, her publisher, and herself. However, she learned to use this failure as a learning opportunity and to not let it define her.

Another challenge Jane faced was the pressure to maintain her success as a poet. She knew that the path to success was not easy and that it required hard work and dedication. She was determined to make the most of her opportunity and to prove to herself and others that she had what it takes to be a successful writer. She was determined to make a name for herself in the literary world and to leave a lasting impact.

Despite these challenges, Jane had learned to overcome adversity. She had learned to never give up on her dreams, to face her fears and to never let setbacks define her. She had become a stronger and more resilient person, and she was proud of all that she had accomplished.

Through her persistence and determination, Jane had achieved her dream and had found her place in the literary world. She had learned that success was not easy, but it was achievable if you were willing to work hard and never give up. She had become a respected and successful poet, and had gained the respect of her peers.

Jane also realized that her journey had not just been about achieving success, but also about the person she had become. She had learned to be more resilient, to never give up, to learn from failure and to overcome adversity. She had become a role model for many aspiring writers and wanted to share her story and her lessons with others.

Overcoming adversity had been a valuable lesson for Jane. She had learned that success was not guaranteed and that it required hard work, dedication, and the ability to rise above challenges and setbacks. She was determined to continue to apply this lesson to her life and to inspire others to do the same. She knew that the journey would not be easy, but she was ready to face whatever challenges lay ahead, with the determination and resilience she had gained along the way.

Chapter 11: The Final Push

Jane had come a long way in her journey as a writer. She had faced many challenges and obstacles, but she had overcome them all. She had learned to never give up on her dreams, to face her fears and to never let setbacks define her. She had become a respected and successful poet, and had gained the respect of her peers. She had published her work in various literary magazines, had been invited to poetry readings and events, and had gained a following of readers who appreciated her work.

Despite her success, Jane knew that there was still more to achieve. She had a vision for her future and knew that the final push was needed to reach it. She had set her sights on publishing a poetry collection, and was determined to make it happen. She wanted to take her poetry to the next level and to reach a wider audience. She wanted to leave a lasting impact and to be remembered as a successful and respected poet.

The final push was not easy. It required hard work, dedication, and the ability to rise above any challenges that came her way. Jane knew that publishing a poetry collection was no small feat and that it would require a significant amount of effort and resources. She had to write new poetry, revise and edit her work, and find a publisher who would take her on. She had to navigate the competitive world of publishing and find a way to stand out.

She spent countless hours writing, revising and editing her poetry, making sure that each and every poem was polished to perfection. She poured over her work and made sure that it was the best it could be. She also had to find a publisher that would take her on, which was a daunting task in itself. She reached out to literary agents, sent her work to various publishers, and attended poetry readings and events in search of opportunities.

Despite the challenges, Jane persisted. She knew that the final push was necessary to achieve her dream, and she was determined to see it through. She faced rejections and setbacks, but she did not let them discourage her. Instead, she used them as motivation to improve her work and to keep pushing forward.

Finally, through her persistence and determination, Jane found a publisher who was interested in her work. Her poetry collection was accepted, and she was finally able to see her vision come to fruition. She had achieved her dream of publishing a poetry collection, and it was a proud moment for her. The book received positive reviews, was well received and was even nominated for literary awards.

The final push had been a valuable lesson for Jane. She had learned that success was not guaranteed and that it required hard work, dedication, and the ability to rise above challenges and setbacks. She had also learned that the journey never truly ends, and that there is always more to achieve and more to strive for. But most importantly, she had learned that with persistence and determination, anything is possible.

Chapter 12: The Triumph of the Human Spirit

Jane's journey as a writer had been a testament to the triumph of the human spirit. She had faced many challenges and obstacles, but she had overcome them all. She had learned to never give up on her dreams, to face her fears and to never let setbacks define her. She had become a respected and successful poet, and had gained the respect of her peers. She had achieved her dream of publishing a poetry collection and received positive reviews, was well received and was even nominated for literary awards.

The triumph of the human spirit had been evident throughout Jane's journey. Despite the rejections, setbacks, and failures, she had never given up on her dream. She had faced her fears and had overcome them. She had faced adversity and had risen above it. She had persevered and had succeeded. She had faced the rejection of her first novel, the pressure to maintain her success as a poet and the struggles of navigating the competitive world of publishing. However, she had used these challenges as an opportunity to learn, to grow and to improve.

Through her journey, Jane had also learned the importance of resilience. She had learned to bounce back from setbacks and to keep moving forward. She had learned to be strong in the face of adversity and to never give up. She had become a role model for many aspiring writers and had inspired others to never give up on their dreams. She had demonstrated that with hard work and determination, anything is possible.

The triumph of the human spirit had also been evident in Jane's personal life. She had faced challenges in her relationships with friends and family, but she had overcome them. She had learned to set boundaries, to communicate effectively and to prioritize her well-being. She had become a stronger and more resilient person, and had found balance in her life. She had worked hard to repair her relationships with friends and family, and to find balance in her life. She had learned that resilience was key to achieving her goals and to finding happiness and fulfillment in her life.

The triumph of the human spirit had been a valuable lesson for Jane. She had learned that success was not guaranteed, and that it required hard work, dedication, and the ability to rise above challenges and setbacks. She had also learned that the journey never truly ends, and that there is always more to achieve and more to strive for. But most importantly, she had learned that with persistence, determination, resilience and the willingness to learn from failures and setbacks, anything is possible.

Jane's journey as a writer had been a testament to the triumph of the human spirit. She had faced many challenges and obstacles, but she had overcome them all. She had achieved her dream and had found her place in the literary world. She had become a respected and successful poet and had inspired others to never give up on their dreams. The triumph of the human spirit had been the driving force behind her journey, and it would continue to be the driving force in her future. She was determined to continue to grow and evolve as a writer and to use her experience to empower others and to show them that with hard work, determination, resilience and the willingness to learn from failure, anything is possible.

Chapter 13: The Aftermath of Victory

Jane had finally achieved her dream of publishing a poetry collection, and it was a proud moment for her. She had overcome many challenges and obstacles, and her hard work and determination had paid off. The book had received positive reviews, was well received, and even nominated for literary awards. She had become a respected and successful poet in the literary world, and had gained the respect of her peers.

However, the aftermath of victory brought its own set of challenges for Jane. She had to navigate the world of literary fame, and learn to handle the attention and expectations that came with it. She had to find a way to balance her newfound success with her personal life and relationships. She had to find a way to continue to create and produce new work, while also maintaining her reputation and legacy.

One of the biggest challenges Jane faced was the pressure to maintain her success. She knew that the literary world was competitive and that it was easy to become a one-hit wonder. She had to continue to produce new and exciting work, while also maintaining her reputation and legacy. She had to find a way to balance her creative process with the expectations of her readers, publishers and critics. To achieve this, she took time to research, study and read other poets and poets of the past, this helped her to understand the literary scene and to develop a sense of where her place was in it. She also took time to reflect on her own writing, looking for ways to improve and evolve.

Another challenge Jane faced was the pressure to live up to her reputation. She had become a respected and successful poet, and she had gained the respect of her peers. She had to find a way to live up to her reputation, while also staying true to herself. She had to find a way to continue to create and produce new work, while also maintaining her integrity and artistic vision. To achieve this, she made sure to keep a journal with her at all times, where she would jot down new ideas, new thoughts and new perspectives. This helped her to stay inspired and to make sure that her work reflected her true self.

Despite these challenges, Jane had learned to navigate the aftermath of victory. She had learned to balance her newfound success with her personal life and relationships. She had learned to continue to create and produce new work, while also maintaining her reputation and legacy. She had learned to live up to her reputation, while also staying true to herself.

The aftermath of victory had been a valuable lesson for Jane. She had learned that success was not the end goal, and that it required hard work, dedication, and the ability to rise above challenges and setbacks. She had also learned that the journey never truly ends, and that there is always more to achieve and more to strive for. But most importantly, she had learned that the aftermath of victory requires a new set of skills and mindset, and with persistence, determination, balance, inspiration and self-reflection, anything is possible.

Jane had finally achieved her dream, and it was a proud moment for her. She had become a respected and successful poet, and had gained the respect of her peers. She was excited

AGAINST ALL ODDS: A NOVEL OF TRIUMPH AND PERSEVERANCE

for what the future held and was determined to continue to grow and evolve as a writer. She was ready for the next step in her journey, and she was excited to see where it would take her. With her newfound skills and mindset, she was confident that she would be able to continue to achieve her goals and to make a lasting impact in the literary world.

Chapter 14: The Legacy of Perseverance

Jane's journey as a writer had been a testament to the power of perseverance. She had faced many challenges and obstacles, but she had never given up on her dream. She had learned to never give up on her dreams, to face her fears and to never let setbacks define her. She had become a respected and successful poet, and had gained the respect of her peers. She had achieved her dream of publishing a poetry collection and had left a lasting impact on the literary world.

The legacy of perseverance had been evident throughout Jane's journey. She had faced rejections, setbacks, and failures, but she had always found a way to keep going. She had never given up on her dream, and she had always found a way to rise above the challenges that had come her way. She had become an inspiration to many aspiring writers, and had shown them that with hard work and determination, anything is possible.

Through her journey, Jane had also learned the importance of perseverance in the face of adversity. She had learned that success is not guaranteed, and that it requires the ability to rise above challenges and setbacks. She had also learned that the journey never truly ends, and that there is always more to achieve and more to strive for. She had become a role model for many aspiring writers and had shown them that with perseverance, anything is possible.

The legacy of perseverance had also been evident in Jane's personal life. She had faced challenges in her relationships with friends and family, but she had never given up on them. She had learned to set boundaries, to communicate effectively and to prioritize her well-being. She had become a stronger and more resilient person, and had found balance in her life. She had shown others that with perseverance, anything is possible.

The legacy of perseverance had been a valuable lesson for Jane. She had learned that success is not guaranteed, and that it requires the ability to rise above challenges and setbacks. She had also learned that the journey never truly ends, and that there is always more to achieve and more to strive for. But most importantly, she had learned that with perseverance, anything is possible.

Jane's journey as a writer had been a testament to the legacy of perseverance. She had faced many challenges and obstacles, but she had never given up on her dream. She had achieved her dream of publishing a poetry collection and had left a lasting impact on the literary world. Her book had become a bestseller and had been translated into multiple languages, reaching readers all around the world. She had become a respected and successful poet, and had gained the respect of her peers. She had inspired many aspiring writers to never give up on their dreams and to persevere in the face of adversity.

The legacy of perseverance had also been evident in Jane's impact on the literary community. She had become an active member of literary organizations, and had used her platform to advocate for underrepresented voices in the literary world. She had also mentored young writers, providing guidance and support to help them achieve their own dreams. She had become a role model for many aspiring writers and had shown them that with hard work, determination, and perseverance, anything is possible.

In conclusion, Jane's journey as a writer had been a testament to the legacy of perseverance. Her story had become an inspiration to many and her legacy would continue to inspire generations of writers to come. She had shown that with hard work, determination, and perseverance, anything is possible and that the human spirit is capable of overcoming any obstacle. Her book had become a classic, and her name was synonymous with perseverance and the triumph of the human spirit.

Chapter 15: The Future of Triumph

Jane's journey as a writer had come to a successful end, but her legacy of triumph and perseverance would live on. She had achieved her dream of publishing a poetry collection and had left a lasting impact on the literary world. She had become a respected and successful poet, and had gained the respect of her peers. She had inspired many aspiring writers to never give up on their dreams and to persevere in the face of adversity.

The future of triumph looked bright for Jane. She had many plans for her future as a writer. She had already begun work on her next poetry collection, with the hope of continuing to inspire and empower others through her writing. She had started to experiment with different styles, forms, and themes in her poetry, to keep her work fresh and exciting. She also planned to release a few poetry books in the coming years, to continue to build her readership and to maintain her reputation as a respected and successful poet.

In addition to her writing, Jane also had plans to use her platform to bring awareness to important social and political issues. She had always been passionate about using her voice for good and now with her platform, she had a greater ability to make a difference in the world. She had begun collaborating with various organizations and non-profits, using her poetry as a tool for education and social change. She also planned to start giving poetry workshops and lectures at schools, libraries and community centers, to empower young people and to inspire them to pursue their own creative passions.

Jane's legacy of triumph and perseverance would continue to inspire generations of writers to come. She had shown that with hard work, determination, and perseverance, anything is possible, and that the human spirit is capable of overcoming any obstacle. Her book had become a classic, and her name was synonymous with perseverance and the triumph of the human spirit.

The future of triumph looked bright for Jane, and she was excited to see where her journey as a writer would take her next. She was determined to continue to grow and evolve as a writer, to use her platform for good, and to continue to inspire and empower others through her writing. She was confident that with her persistence, determination, and perseverance, she would continue to achieve her goals and to make a lasting impact in the literary world.

The future of triumph was in her hands, and she was ready to take on the challenges that came her way, with courage, determination and perseverance. Her journey as a writer had been a shining example of what it meant to triumph against all odds and her legacy would live on as a testament to the power of human spirit.

About the Publisher

Accepting manuscripts in the most categories. We love to help people get their words available to the world.

Revival Waves of Glory focus is to provide more options to be published. We do traditional paperbacks, hardcovers, audio books and ebooks all over the world. A traditional royalty-based publisher that offers self-publishing options, Revival Waves provides a very author friendly and transparent publishing process, with President Bill Vincent involved in the full process of your book. Send us your manuscript and we will contact you as soon as possible.

Contact: Bill Vincent at rwgpublishing@yahoo.com

CPSIA information can be obtained
at www.ICGtesting.com
Printed in the USA
BVHW040251130523
664067BV00002B/493